BATTLING COVID-19
Financial FREE FALL
The COVID-19 Economic Crisis

MARIE BENDER

Checkerboard Library

An Imprint of Abdo Publishing
abdobooks.com

abdobooks.com

Published by Abdo Publishing, a division of ABDO, PO Box 398166, Minneapolis, Minnesota 55439. Copyright © 2021 by Abdo Consulting Group, Inc. International copyrights reserved in all countries. No part of this book may be reproduced in any form without written permission from the publisher. Checkerboard Library™ is a trademark and logo of Abdo Publishing.

Printed in the United States of America, North Mankato, Minnesota
102020
012021

Design: Sarah DeYoung, Mighty Media, Inc.
Production: Mighty Media, Inc.
Editor: Jessica Rusick
Cover Photograph: Shutterstock Images
Interior Photographs: Dan Keck/Flickr, p. 11; Edwin Wriston/The National Guard/Flickr, p. 28; Flickr, p. 15; Joe Raedle/Getty Images, p. 21; Mark Lennihan/AP Images, p. 9; Nati Harnik/AP Images, p. 17; Open Grid Scheduler Grid Engine/Flickr, p. 7; Pat Sutphin/AP Images, p. 19; Shutterstock Images, pp. 5, 6, 13, 24, 25, 27; The White House/Flickr, pp. 6 (top right), 23
Design Elements: Shutterstock Images

Library of Congress Control Number: 2020940240

Publisher's Cataloging-in-Publication Data
Names: Bender, Marie, author.
Title: Financial free fall: The COVID-19 economic crisis / by Marie Bender
Other title: The COVID-19 economic crisis
Description: Minneapolis, Minnesota : Abdo Publishing, 2021 | Series: Battling COVID-19 | Includes online resources and index
Identifiers: ISBN 9781532194276 (lib. bdg.) | ISBN 9781098213633 (ebook)
Subjects: LCSH: COVID-19 (Disease)--Juvenile literature. | Economics--Juvenile literature. | Finance, Personal--Juvenile literature. | Unemployment--Social aspects--Juvenile literature. | Business losses—Juvenile literature.
Classification: DDC 330--dc23

Contents

The COVID-19 Pandemic 4

Timeline 6

Stock Market Falls 8

Restaurant Restrictions 10

Retail Reduction 12

Farms and Food 16

Record Unemployment 20

Government Stimulus.......................... 22

Global Impact 24

Reopening the Economy 26

Glossary 30

Online Resources 31

Index.. 32

The COVID-19 Pandemic

In late 2019, people in Wuhan, China, started getting sick with a new disease. The disease became known as COVID-19. Within a few months, COVID-19 spread around the world. On March 11, 2020, the **World Health Organization (WHO)** declared COVID-19 a **pandemic**.

The coronavirus that causes COVID-19 passes easily from person to person. To slow the spread of COVID-19, world governments told people to practice social distancing. This meant avoiding large crowds and staying at least six feet (2 m) away from others in public places. In the United States, most states issued orders for residents to stay at home.

Over time, social distancing and stay-at-home orders slowed the spread of COVID-19. However, they also caused a lot of restaurants, factories, and stores to close. Millions of people lost their jobs. This affected every aspect of the economy. Many people felt the effects of a financial free fall.

WHAT IS A CORONAVIRUS?

Coronaviruses are a large group of viruses that cause **respiratory** illnesses. Most coronaviruses exist only in animals. However, several have spread from animals to humans. The coronavirus discovered in Wuhan is called severe acute respiratory syndrome coronavirus 2 (SARS-CoV-2). It causes a disease called coronavirus disease 2019, or COVID-19. COVID-19 spreads when saliva droplets pass from person to person. This can happen when someone coughs, sneezes, sings, breathes, or talks. Most people with COVID-19 do not suffer serious **symptoms**. But some people develop life-threatening problems. Because of this, the virus is viewed as a threat to world health.

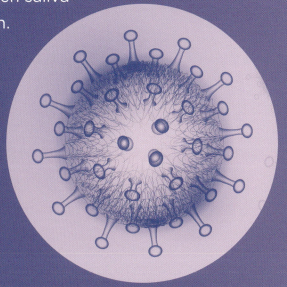

TIMELINE

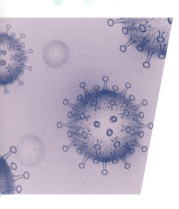

LATE 2019

A new disease emerges in Wuhan, China. It is later named COVID-19.

MARCH 27, 2020

President Trump signs the Coronavirus Aid, Relief, and Economic Security (CARES) Act. It gives money to businesses and individuals who are struggling during the pandemic.

MARCH 11, 2020

The World Health Organization (WHO) declares COVID-19 a pandemic.

APRIL 1, 2020

In the United States, about 30,000 restaurants have closed permanently due to the COVID-19 pandemic.

APRIL 7, 2020

Most US states are under stay-at-home orders.

MID-JUNE 2020

Many states have begun reopening.

JULY 2020

COVID-19 cases rise sharply in some states where businesses have reopened.

APRIL 23, 2020

Congress passes a stimulus package called the Paycheck Protection Program and Health Care Enhancement Act.

LATE OCTOBER 2020

The US has more than 8 million COVID-19 cases. More than 220,000 people have died.

Stock Market Falls

The US **stock** market was one of the first institutions affected by the COVID-19 **crisis.** The stock market is where investors buy and sell stock in different companies. Investors try to buy stock when the price is low. Then, they sell it when the price goes up.

High stock prices are a sign of a strong economy. It means the country's businesses are profitable and growing. Small stock price decreases happen often. However, the prices usually go back up quickly. This does not affect the economy.

If stock prices suddenly decrease by a lot, the economy could be in trouble. Stock prices can fall if investors believe companies are not going to make money. Concerned investors will try to quickly sell stock before the stock loses value. And, investors won't buy new stock. This causes the stock market to fall.

In February and March 2020, investors worried about the effect of COVID-19 on businesses. Their fears caused the stock market to fall by 30 percent. This drop has been likened to the 1929 stock market crash that led to the **Great Depression**.

Traders at the New York Stock Exchange watch President Donald Trump give a COVID-19 press conference on March 18, 2020.

Responses by government officials and the **Federal Reserve System** helped **stock** market prices rise slightly. But the economy couldn't fully recover until businesses could reopen.

Restaurant Restrictions

Restaurants were some of the first businesses affected by COVID-19. Restaurant tables are often arranged close to one another. So, it was easy for COVID-19 to spread among people dining in a restaurant. In the middle of March 2020, many US restaurants closed their dining areas for safety.

However, many restaurants still offered curbside pickup. Customers placed to-go orders online or over the phone. Then, they picked up the food outside the restaurant. People could also order food to their homes. And, most fast-food restaurants were open for drive-through service.

STEM CONNECTION

Some restaurants stopped accepting cash during the COVID-19 **pandemic**. That's because viruses like SARS-CoV-2 can survive for multiple days on paper money. Cashless restaurants asked customers to pay using other methods. These included credit cards or smartphone apps.

In the first three months of the pandemic, the nation's restaurants lost an estimated $120 billion in sales.

To help restaurants survive, loyal customers ordered take-out meals as much as possible. But restaurants still lost a lot of business. Many closed. According to the National Restaurant Association, three percent of US restaurants closed permanently by April 1, 2020. That's about 30,000 restaurants. Some experts believed that 20 percent of US restaurants could close before the COVID-19 **pandemic** was over.

Retail Reduction

Restaurants were not the only businesses affected by the COVID-19 crisis. By April 7, most US states were under stay-at-home orders. These orders required all but **essential** businesses to close.

Essential stores varied from state to state. But grocery stores and **pharmacies** were commonly considered essential. This is because they sold items people needed most. These items included food, medicine, and cleaning supplies.

By early April, more than 190,000 US businesses had closed due to COVID-19. In some cases, customers could order products online and have their purchases delivered. Businesses also offered curbside pickup. Even so, many suffered. Experts estimated some retail companies would lose 90 percent of their **revenues**.

Many stores that remained open made changes to follow social distancing guidelines. These changes included closing earlier than usual. This gave employees time to clean and **sanitize** the stores before opening the next day. Many stores also **restricted** the number of customers who could be inside at one time.

US STAY-AT-HOME ORDERS

BY MARCH 23

- California
- Connecticut
- Illinois
- Louisiana
- New Jersey
- New York
- Ohio
- Oregon
- Washington

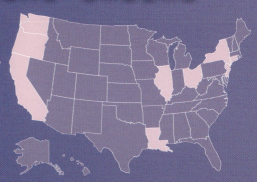

BY MARCH 30

- Alaska
- Colorado
- Delaware
- Hawaii
- Idaho
- Indiana
- Kansas
- Kentucky
- Maryland
- Massachusetts
- Michigan
- Minnesota
- Montana
- New Hampshire
- New Mexico
- North Carolina
- Rhode Island
- Vermont
- Virginia
- Washington, DC
- West Virginia
- Wisconsin

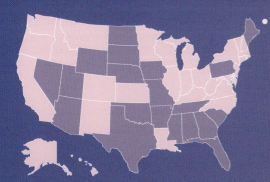

BY APRIL 7

- Alabama
- Arizona
- Florida
- Georgia
- Maine
- Mississippi
- Missouri
- Nevada
- Pennsylvania
- South Carolina
- Tennessee
- Texas

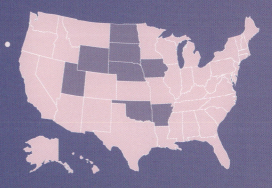

NO STATEWIDE ORDERS

- Arkansas
- Iowa
- Nebraska
- North Dakota
- Oklahoma
- South Dakota
- Utah
- Wyoming

And, they offered special shopping hours for some shoppers. These shoppers had a higher risk of developing a serious case of COVID-19. Among those at risk were older people and people with certain medical conditions.

Some stores were having financial trouble even before the COVID-19 **pandemic**. Online shopping had become increasingly popular. So already, fewer people were going into stores to shop. Some stores couldn't survive being closed for months. They were forced to close permanently.

EMPTY SHELVES

At first, people didn't know how long stay-at-home orders would last. So, shoppers stocked up on food and supplies. Often, people bought more than they needed. This caused stores to run out of popular items. Hand **sanitizer** and cleaning spray quickly sold out. That's because they help stop the spread of the SARS-CoV-2 virus. Toilet paper was another product that sold faster than stores could restock it. From mid-March to the end of April, very few stores had toilet paper. Stores that did have toilet paper often limited how much each customer could buy.

Stickers placed six feet (2 m) apart on floors told customers where to stand to practice social distancing.

Farms and Food

The COVID-19 **pandemic** also affected farms and food production. One effect was reduced demand for farm products. Many farmers normally sold their meats, produce, dairy products, and eggs to schools and restaurants. However, many of these places closed during the pandemic. So, farmers had extra food they couldn't sell.

At grocery stores, demand for food was high. With restaurants closed, people bought more food to prepare at home. Farmers also sold food to grocery stores. However, these sales weren't enough to make up for the loss of sales to schools and restaurants.

While some people stocked up at grocery stores, others had trouble getting enough food. People who lost their jobs had less

CORPORATE CONTRIBUTIONS

Food and beverage company PepsiCo was one of many large companies that helped those affected by COVID-19. PepsiCo spent more than $45 million to help communities worldwide. The money provided meals to hungry people. It also provided aid to jobless restaurant workers.

In Omaha, Nebraska, the Together food pantry helped run a drive-through food pantry for those in need.

money to spend on food. Many children also relied on school lunches for meals. With schools closed, families lost this source of food. Food assistance organizations were overwhelmed with requests for help.

STEM CONNECTION

Many US meatpacking plants have been affected by COVID-19 outbreaks. One reason is that meatpacking plants are kept very cold. This keeps the meat from spoiling. But cold air may help viruses like SARS-CoV-2 survive outside the human body. Research suggests cold air hardens the virus's outer layer. This makes the virus more durable and allows it to spread more easily.

Many farmers **donated** extra produce to these programs. However, the organizations had limited refrigerators to store the food. This meant they could not take **perishable** items such as milk or eggs. Some farmers had to destroy millions of pounds of food because they couldn't sell or donate it.

Food packaging plants were also affected by COVID-19. Many plants were set up to package food specifically for restaurants and schools. When schools and restaurants closed, many plants had to close too. Lack of employees also affected food production and packaging. COVID-19 **outbreaks** made many employees sick. Many plants had to slow production or close because fewer people were able to work.

US farmers were forced to dump out millions of gallons of unused milk during the pandemic.

Record Unemployment

Workers across the United States felt the effects of the COVID-19 **crisis.** In February 2020, the US unemployment rate was at 3.5 percent. This means only 3.5 percent of Americans who were able to work were without jobs. This was the lowest unemployment rate in 50 years! But by the end of April, the COVID-19 **pandemic** had left more than 20 million people jobless. The nation's unemployment rate had risen to 14.7 percent. This was the highest it had been since the **Great Depression**.

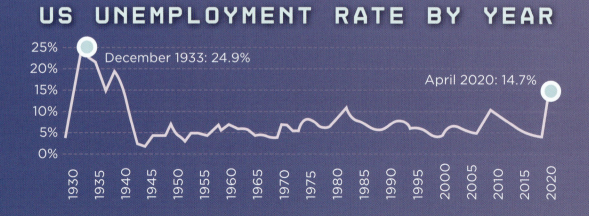

In Hialeah, Florida, officials handed out printed unemployment applications when the state's website failed.

When US citizens lose their jobs, they can apply for state unemployment benefits. This gives them money while they look for a new job. By the end of April, tens of millions of Americans had applied for unemployment benefits.

Most states were unprepared to handle so many applications. Websites crashed when people applied online. Phone lines were busy when people called to ask questions. And, processing and approving applications was delayed.

States began to run out of money. So, many had to borrow money from the federal government's unemployment fund. President Trump also signed the Coronavirus Aid, Relief, and Economic Security (CARES) Act on March 27. One part of the CARES Act provided additional money for unemployed people.

Government Stimulus

The CARES Act was one of several **stimulus** packages the US government passed during the COVID-19 **pandemic.** Its provisions included $500 billion in loans for businesses, cities, and states. This money helped keep businesses open. And, the CARES Act gave $1,200 to US adults who earned less than $75,000 per year. Families received an additional $500 for each child.

Another stimulus package passed on April 23. It was called the Paycheck Protection Program and Health Care Enhancement Act. It included $310 billion to help businesses pay employees' salaries. The act also gave $75 billion to hospitals and healthcare providers. This helped provide equipment and medicines to treat COVID-19 patients.

The aid from these packages helped many people and businesses survive the early months of the COVID-19 pandemic. But the packages were not a permanent solution.

President Trump signs the CARES Act.

Government officials had to figure out how to let businesses safely reopen. Only then could the economy start to improve.

Global Impact

GERMANY

Germany's unemployment rate rose less quickly than the unemployment rates of many other countries. That's because the German government helped companies pay portions of employees' salaries. This kept millions of people from losing their jobs.

MEXICO

Mexico's economy was facing a downturn before the **pandemic**. The COVID-19 **crisis** made things worse. Many businesses depended on foreign tourists to make money. However, fewer people traveled during the pandemic. In response to the crisis, the Mexican government provided small loans to some individuals and businesses.

CHINA

China was the first country to close **nonessential** businesses in response to COVID-19. By the end of March, up to 80 million Chinese citizens were estimated to be out of work. On May 22, the Chinese government introduced a $500 billion **stimulus** package. The package would help create new jobs.

INDIA

India's economy faced a harsh downturn during the **pandemic**. Most businesses closed in March to stop COVID-19's spread. In April, the country's unemployment rate rose to 27 percent. This was the highest it had ever been. In May, the Indian government passed a stimulus package of more than $250 billion to help the country's economy.

Reopening the Economy

Most US government officials and health experts agreed that closing the economy was necessary to slow the spread of COVID-19. But there were disagreements about how long the shutdown should last. Some people felt that the financial cost of closing the economy was worse than the effects of COVID-19. Others wanted to ensure COVID-19 was under control before reopening businesses.

SHUTDOWN PROTESTS

Polls showed most Americans supported the stay-at-home orders issued by US governors. However, there were protests against the shutdowns in many states. People protested for various reasons. Some thought it was unfair that many small businesses had to close. Other protesters believed the government had gone too far in telling people where they could and couldn't go.

To help customers practice social distancing, reopened restaurants spaced their tables at least six feet (2 m) apart.

Plans for reopening varied from state to state. Some states started reopening in late April. Others waited longer. Some states only let certain types of businesses open. Others let businesses open only if they were in areas with few COVID-19 cases. By mid-June, many states were at least partly open.

The **Centers for Disease Control and Prevention (CDC)** provided recommendations to help businesses reopen safely. The recommendations included limiting the number of people

27

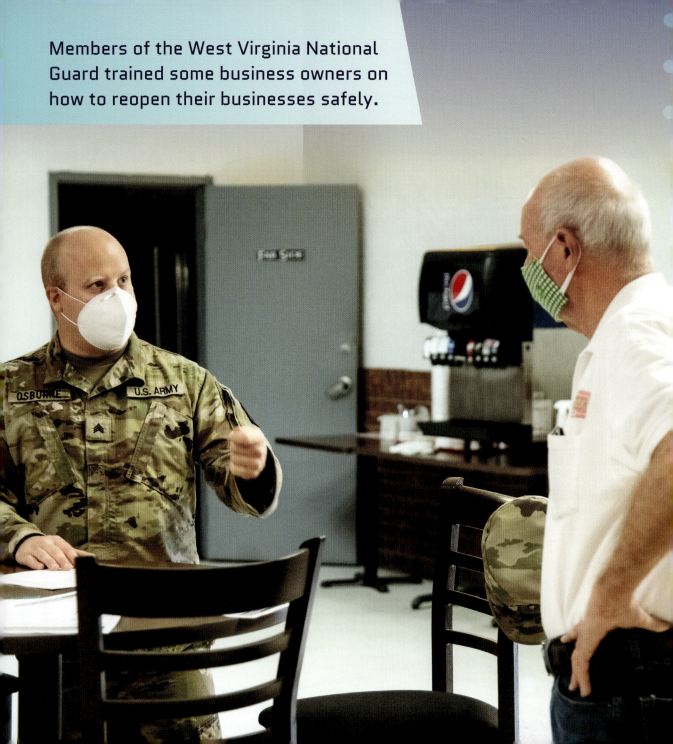

Members of the West Virginia National Guard trained some business owners on how to reopen their businesses safely.

allowed into stores and restaurants at one time. The **CDC** also encouraged people to stay six feet (2 m) apart and wear face masks in public.

Although businesses could reopen, COVID-19 was still a threat. Many people were still concerned about catching the virus. So, they continued to stay away from crowded places. But other people resumed activities such as shopping and eating out.

Throughout July, new COVID-19 cases rose sharply in some states where businesses reopened. These states included California, Texas, and Florida. Governors in these states ordered businesses to close again.

Cases began to decline in several states during the early fall. But by late September, cases were rising across the country once again. By late October, the US had more than 8 million COVID-19 cases. More than 220,000 had been fatal. Across the nation, it was clear that economic recovery would be a slow process.

STEM CONNECTION

Face masks are worn over the nose and mouth. They help contain droplets that can spread COVID-19. During the **pandemic**, many people made their own face masks from cloth.

Glossary

Centers for Disease Control and Prevention (CDC)—the main national health organization in the United States. The CDC works to control the spread of disease and maintain and improve public health in the United States and other countries.

crisis—a difficult or dangerous situation that needs serious attention.

donate—to give.

essential—very important or necessary. Something that is not essential is nonessential.

Federal Reserve System—the central bank of the United States.

Great Depression—the period from 1929 to 1942 of worldwide economic trouble. There was little buying or selling, and many people could not find work.

outbreak—a sudden increase in the occurrence of an illness.

pandemic—worldwide spread of a disease that can affect most people.

perishable—likely to go bad or spoil quickly.

pharmacy—a store in which drugs are made and sold.

respiratory—having to do with the system of organs involved with breathing.

restrict—to keep within certain limits.

revenue—the total income produced from a given source.

sanitize—to make something free from disease by cleaning it. Sanitizer is something that sanitizes.

stimulus—something that encourages growth or activity.

stock—one of many equal parts a business is divided into. People who purchase stock own part of the company.

symptom—a noticeable change in the normal working of the body. A symptom indicates or accompanies disease, sickness, or another malfunction.

World Health Organization (WHO)—an agency of the United Nations that works to maintain and improve the health of people around the world.

Online Resources

To learn more about the COVID-19 pandemic, please visit **abdobooklinks.com** or scan this QR code. These links are routinely monitored and updated to provide the most current information available.

Index

Centers for Disease Control and
  Prevention (CDC), 27, 29
China, 4, 5, 25
closures, 4, 10, 11, 12, 14, 16, 18, 25, 29
Coronavirus Aid, Relief, and Economic
  Security (CARES) Act, 21, 22
curbside pickup, 10, 12

economy, 4, 8, 9, 21, 23, 24, 25, 26, 29

face masks, 29
factories, 4
farms, 16, 18
Federal Reserve System, 9
food assistance, 16, 17, 18
food packaging plants, 18

Germany, 24
Great Depression, 8, 20

high-risk groups, 14

India, 25

Mexico, 24

National Restaurant Association, 11

Paycheck Protection Program and
  Health Care Enhancement Act, 22

reopening, 9, 23, 26, 27, 29
restaurants, 4, 10, 11, 12, 16, 18, 27, 29

SARS-CoV-2 virus, 4, 5, 10, 14, 18, 29
schools, 16, 17, 18
social distancing, 4, 12
stay-at-home orders, 4, 12, 13, 14, 26
stimulus packages, 22, 25
stock market, 8, 9
stores, 4, 12, 14, 16, 27, 29

Trump, Donald, 21

unemployment, 4, 20, 21, 24, 25

World Health Organization (WHO), 4